Bernard Waber

A Lion Named Shirley Williamson

HOUGHTON MIFFLIN COMPANY BOSTON 1996

for Ethel

Walter Lorraine 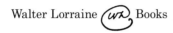 Books

Copyright © 1996 by Bernard Waber

All rights reserved. For information about permission to
reproduce selections from this book, write to Permissions,
Houghton Mifflin Company, 215 Park Avenue South,
New York, New York 10003.

For information about this and other Houghton Mifflin trade
and reference books and multimedia products, visit The Bookstore
at Houghton Mifflin on the World Wide Web at
http://www.hmco.com/trade/.

Library of Congress Cataloging-in-Publication Data

Waber, Bernard.
  A lion named Shirley Williamson / Bernard Waber.
    p. cm.
  Summary: Although a lion's unusual name causes confusion and
misunderstanding at the zoo, she becomes a favorite with
the public and with Seymour the zookeeper.
  ISBN 0-395-80979-7
  [1. Lions—Fiction.   2. Zoo animals—Fiction.   3. Zoos—Fiction.]
I. Title.
PZ7.W113Li   1996
[E]—dc20   96-11187
                                                               CIP
                                                                AC

Printed in the United States of America

WOZ   10   9   8   7   6   5   4   3   2   1

Once there was a lion named Shirley Williamson.
"But that's ridiculous," said some of the visitors to the zoo,
"she doesn't even look like a Shirley Williamson."
"Nor does she behave like a Shirley Williamson,"
they quickly added, when Shirley roared at them.

The other lions, whose names were Goobah, Poobah, and
Aroobah, resented Shirley. They thought she put on airs
and enjoyed special privileges because her name was
Shirley Williamson. They showed their feelings by growling
at her and giving her nasty looks.

Nor was it helpful that Seymour, the zookeeper, served
Shirley her meals on a tray.
"But what am I to do?" said Seymour. "I just can't shove food
at her — not at someone named Shirley Williamson."

And once, because he thought it would please her,
Seymour placed a beautiful rose on Shirley's tray.
Seymour loved kidding around with Shirley.
He thought she had a terrific sense of humor for a lion.

Seymour even began adding little homey touches to
Shirley's cage — like leafy plants and a cheerful little rug for
her to recline upon when she was exhausted from roaring.
"This would never be happening if her name weren't
Shirley Williamson," the other lions unhappily agreed.

So how did it happen that Shirley Williamson was named
Shirley Williamson in the first place?
It all began when a recently captured lion was about to be
shipped to the city zoo. A woman working at the
Wildlife Trading Company telephoned the zoo
to confirm shipment.

"Hello," the woman began cheerily, "we have a shipping
order here for one lioness. Will you accept delivery?"

"Most certainly," said the delighted zoo director.

"Oh, by the way," he asked, "does the lion have a name?"
Because of a faulty connection the woman mistakenly
thought she was asked for her own name.

"Shirley Williamson," she answered.

"Shirley Williamson! Heh-heh-heh," the director chuckled,
"that sure is a weird name…"

And before he could add the words "for a lion," the woman
said, "Sir!!!! I'll have you know Shirley Williamson is a
beautiful, decent, respected name, and don't you forget it.
Whatever happened to good manners!" she muttered,
slamming down the receiver.

Click!!!!

"Huh!" said the director. "All I said was Shirley
Williamson is a weird name for a lion. Was that so terrible?
Was that a reason to get huffy? So the lion's name is Shirley
Williamson, good! I have no problem with it."

But there were problems. No sooner was Shirley installed at
the zoo when complaints began coming in left and right
from people named Shirley Williamson. They didn't like
sharing their name with a ferocious animal.
And once, eight women and one man, each named Shirley
Williamson, stormed into the director's office demanding
to be heard.

To make it up to them, the director invited everyone named Shirley Williamson to enjoy a free day at the zoo. He proclaimed it Shirley Williamson Day.

But when the newspapers got hold of the story, this small event blossomed into an enormous celebration, with tributes all around for everyone everywhere named Shirley Williamson. It was a huge success.

It also made Shirley Williamson, the lion, famous. Overnight, she began drawing visitors to the zoo in big numbers. Shirley Williamson was on everyone's "must-see" list. And Shirley never disappointed her fans. She always threw in a few extra roars just to make sure everyone went home happy.

Because of Shirley, business at the zoo zoomed. The gift shop couldn't keep up with demands for Shirley Williamson T-shirts.

And sacks of mail addressed to Shirley Williamson arrived daily. Shirley smiled as Seymour read aloud flattering letters from her numerous fans.

And when Shirley smiled, Seymour smiled.

Seymour couldn't explain, not even to himself, why he enjoyed pleasing Shirley so much — unless, perhaps, it was because his wife, whom he had adored with all of his heart and soul during her lifetime, was also named Shirley.

But Shirley could not always appreciate Seymour's perky
cheerfulness. There were times when she needed to be
alone — alone with sad but cherished memories of her life in
Africa. A life she dearly missed.

And what she most desperately missed, of course,
was freedom — freedom to go here, there, everywhere —
no questions asked.

And she missed independence — hunting for her own food.
But Shirley had her rules: She only hunted when she was
hungry, never for the mere sport of it.

She missed treasured places,

and familiar faces.

She missed the sounds of freedom: the humming,
the buzzing.
She missed long, lazy afternoons, sweetly snoozing
with her family.
She missed keeping a doting, but watchful, eye on the
pride's rowdy cubs.
She missed nuzzling. She missed nibbling. She missed
snuggling.
She missed playful swats and pats. And oh how she
missed having her face and ears roundly washed.
She missed…she missed…she missed home.

"We have a major problem," the zoo director announced one day. "Shirley is getting the lion's share of attention, so to speak. She's been good for the zoo, but not good for the other lions. They are old-timers here and feel entitled to a little respect. Something must be done."

"It's her name that draws attention," said an assistant.
"Yes," said the director, "I hate doing it, but let's change her name. Let's change it to something sensible, something that sounds lion, something like Bingo, Bango, Bongo. That sort of sound. Do you know what I mean?"
"I like Bongo," said the assistant.

"Bongo, Bongo...give me a minute to get used to it...
I just got used to it," said the director. "Yes, let's change her name to Bongo. And we can also do without Seymour.
This will be a far, far happier zoo without Seymour."

The worst part of getting fired, for Seymour, was saying
good-bye to Shirley — now Bongo.
"Listen to me," he advised her, "just go out there and be the best
lion named Bongo you know how to be. That's how to handle it.
But as far as I am concerned — me personally, and the rest of the
world — you will always be Shirley Williamson.
Good-bye, Shirley," he said. "Try to be happy."

When they heard about it, the other lions were jubilant.
"Bongo! It's a scream!" they guffawed, exchanging
revengeful smirks and glances.
"Bongo! Bongo! Bongo!" They took turns mouthing the new,
delightfully loathsome name. Shirley's humiliation gave
them a sense of kinship they had never before enjoyed.

Overnight, the former Shirley Williamson's world crumbled
to her feet — or paws.
"First they took away my freedom, and now they have taken
away my good name," she thought, bemoaning her fate.

One night the new keeper, who, as it happened, was
the director's first cousin and was already making big
mistakes on the job, forgot to close Bongo's cage.
FORGOT TO CLOSE THE CAGE!!!!!
Suddenly, during his break, just as he was about to bite
into a delicious salami sandwich, he remembered.

Too late.
Bongo
(also known as
Shirley Williamson)
was gone.

News of a lion's escape from the zoo
made banner headlines.

On radio, they talked of nothing else.
Bongo, a.k.a. Shirley Williamson,
"WANTED" notices were posted everywhere.

Schools closed.
Office buildings were evacuated.
Taxis, buses, and subways were empty.
Police cars patrolled deserted streets.

Business in restaurants and places of entertainment
went from bad to terrible.
Wild rumors of lion sightings were rampant.
The city was in turmoil.
Where's Bongo? Where's Bongo?
Those words were on everyone's lips.

"Where's Shirley? Where's Shirley?" Seymour repeated,
pacing his living room. He was about to say it again when,
suddenly, he heard scratching at the door.

Seymour's heart pounded as he tiptoed to the door.
Could it be…? No, impossible, he reassured himself.
Seymour opened the door ever so slightly.
But it was — it was SHIRLEY!
Shirley the hunter had hunted down Seymour's house
in Brooklyn. Seymour quickly shut the door.

Seymour heard Shirley whimper. He heard the
loneliness in her voice. Seymour knew all about loneliness.
But she was, after all, a lion — maybe even
a very hungry lion.

He peeked out again at Shirley. She looked back at him
with those sorrowful eyes that never failed to pull at his heart.

Seymour knew he shouldn't, but he opened the door.
Shirley flew into the house. She swiftly explored the room,
glancing at him from time to time as if to say, "So this is
where you live, Seymour — not bad, not bad at all."
She looked here, she looked there, she looked everywhere.

Seymour couldn't believe what was happening.
A wild animal was in his living room, the very room
where his beloved wife once did needlepoint.

Next, Shirley turned her full attention on Seymour.
Seymour froze. Only his eyes moved, and they were
riveted on Shirley.

Shirley inched toward him.
"No, Shirley, please, not too close! Not too close," he
pleaded. "It's me, Seymour, remember? Your best friend at
the zoo? Remember our good times together?
Remember how it was always Shirley and Seymour?"

Suddenly the doorbell rang.
Shirley looked startled as Seymour quickly stepped outside.
It was Mrs. Tobias, his next-door neighbor.
"Here, Seymour," she said, "I made a pot roast for you.
You'll like it. I used your wife's recipe —
may she rest in peace."
"Thank you, Mrs. Tobias. You're always so generous,"
said Seymour.

"Aren't you going to invite me in?" said Mrs. Tobias.
"In!" said Seymour. "You mean, into the house? Now?"
"If you're having company, Seymour, I understand."
"Yes, company," said Seymour. "That's it. Just dropped in.
Big surprise. Big, big surprise, believe me."

"It's all right," said Mrs. Tobias. "I'd rather be home, anyway. Oh, Seymour," she went on, "I'm shaking and quaking about this escaped lion. Last night, I looked under my bed five times. Just talking about it scares me stiff. I have to go. Good night, Seymour. At least you have company."

"Good night, Mrs. Tobias. Thanks again," said Seymour.

Seymour's first thought was to run away, but he returned,
instead, with the pot roast. A look in Shirley's eyes warned
him to put it down at once. With a swoop and two gulps the
pot roast vanished even the little potatoes and carrots.
Seymour stared at the empty pan as Shirley lapped
up the last drops of gravy.

"You didn't want me to warm it up first?"
Seymour struggled for something to say.

With her hunger satisfied,
Shirley was back to her old self.
Even Seymour relaxed a little.
She found a ball of yarn, and began chasing it.
"Shirley, this isn't like you," said Seymour.

But Shirley wasn't listening.
Instead, she rolled on her back, waving her paws
playfully in the air.
"Shirley, if you are pretending to be a cute little house pet,
I'm afraid you have come to the wrong house," said Seymour.

But Shirley wasn't listening.
Instead, she rubbed against Seymour's leg,
purred, and looked up at him adoringly.
"Shirley, Shirley, Shirley! Listen to me, Shirley.
You are a lion, a majestic creature.
To thine own self be true," said Seymour.

But Shirley wasn't listening.
Instead, she licked Seymour's face.
"Ugh! Yecch! Stop! Stop it, Shirley!" cried Seymour.

"Shirley, are you trying to tell me you want to stay here
with me?" said Seymour. "Is that what this is all about?"
The gleam in Shirley's eyes answered, "Yes, yes, yes."

Seymour sighed. "Ah — if only it were possible," he said,
"but people around here — well, they tend to get edgy
about lions. Do you know what I mean?
This is Brooklyn, Shirley — barking yes, roaring no.
But most important — you are not mine to keep.
We have no choice, Shirley. You must go back to the zoo."

But how to get her there?
Seymour found,
still hanging in the closet,
his wife's favorite hat and cloak.

"Life at the zoo...well, let's look at it this way," said
Seymour, in the taxi. "You can always count on having
a roof over your head, meals served on time, a doctor
when you need one. It's not altogether something
to turn up your nose at, kiddo."
This really made Shirley angry, especially when he
called her kiddo. She gave him a fierce look and spent
the rest of the trip staring out the window.

Seymour was immediately sorry.
"Do you know what I wish?" he said. "I wish I could wave
a wand that would magically transport you back to your
homeland — that's what I wish, Shirley."

But Shirley wasn't listening. They traveled in silence,
stopping once so Seymour could make a telephone call.

When they reached the dark entrance to the zoo,
Seymour and Shirley got out of the taxi.
The gates swung open.
Shirley hesitated.
"Go, Shirley," said Seymour. "It will be all right.
They are expecting you."

Shirley walked into the zoo. The cloak and hat slipped
to the ground.
Seymour picked them up and pressed
them to his heart.
"Shirley," he called after her, "my wife would have liked
you, too. She would have adored you, Shirley.
That much I know for a fact."

"Shir-ley! Shir-ley!" the crowds chanted the next day.
Everyone was so happy to see Shirley Williamson again.
They absolutely refused to call her Bongo. Some even
waved placards reading *Shirley Yes, Bongo No.*

"The people have spoken," said the director. "Shirley
will keep the name Shirley Williamson."
"And I have a happy solution for the other lions," beamed
an assistant. "Let's change their names as well."
"To what?" asked the director.
"How about Ralph Weinstock, Harvey Johnson, and
Sylvester J. Hotchkiss, Jr.?" the assistant answered.

"Wherever did you get those names?" said the director.
"From the telephone book," the assistant answered proudly.
"Let me think about it," said the director. "In the meantime, we
should re-hire Seymour. Seymour never left cage doors open."

"Shir-ley! Shir-ley!" everyone kept chanting.
And in the center of the crowd, smiling, waving,
and giving thumbs-up signs, stood Seymour.
When Shirley saw Seymour, she gave him the biggest,
warmest, happiest roar of all.